A
SPRING
STORY

by David Updike

illustrations by

Robert Andrew Parker

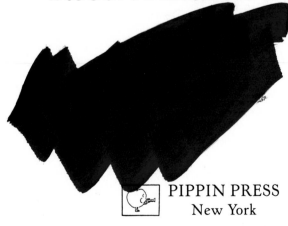

PIPPIN PRESS
New York

Published by Pippin Press, 229 East 85th Street,
Gracie Station Box #92, New York, N.Y. 10028

Printed in Spain by Novograph, S. A., Madrid   .J

10 9 8 7 6 5 4 3 2 1

Library of Congress Cataloging-in-Publication Data

Updike, David.
  A spring story/by David Updike ; illustrations by Robert Andrew
Parker.
    p.   cm.
  Summary: Homer, his dog Sophocles, and friend Henry have fun
riding an iceberg down the creek until rushing waters threaten to
take them out to sea.
  ISBN 0-945912-06-4 :
  [1. Icebergs—Fiction. 2. Spring—Fiction.] I. Parker, Robert
Andrew, ill. II. Title.
PZ7.U458Sp 1989
[E]—dc19
                                                    89-8450
                                                      CIP
                                                       AC

For Michael Kwame

A
SPRING
STORY

It had been the coldest winter in forty years, and the marsh and the creek were still frozen, covered with a vast sheet of ice and snow. Homer had made a new friend at school that year, a boy named Henry, and together they would explore the woods and fields, and take long walks together out across the frozen marsh—running, sliding, jumping over creeks and canals and climbing onto the enormous icebergs, two feet thick, which had washed up with the flood tide. Henry was about the same age as Homer, (three days older) and was about the same weight and height, and had a dog, too, named Max, who would run out before them with Sophocles, chasing after the scent of a deer or scaring the ducks and geese that came to rest on their long journey north for the summer.

But toward the end of March, there were signs of spring. The days began slowly to warm, and lengthen; birds sang down from the budding trees, a warm, yellow sun shone down from a soft blue sky, and enormous icebergs, two feet thick, drifted in and out of the creek with the rising and falling tides. One afternoon, on one of their walks, Homer and Henry met an old man who lived in a small, white house on the edge of the marsh. He was tall and thin, and wore a tired old baseball cap, and was carrying in his arms a load of driftwood he had collected from the marsh.

"Good afternoon, boys," he said when he saw them. "Nice day for a walk, isn't it? What's your dog's name?" he asked, bending down to pet their heads.

"This is Sophocles." Homer said.

"And this is Max." Henry added.

"And I'm Mr. Birch." the man said, reaching out to shake the two boys' hands. "But you can call me Ralph."

"I'm Henry." Henry said.

"And I'm Homer."

"Well, pleased to meet you both. I've seen you from a distance, but we never did get a chance to meet." he said, and then looked off toward the horizon and laughed softly. "It's been a long, cold winter, but I guess its about over for now. Why, I remember when I was about your age we had another cold winter like this—colder, even—and in the spring we were running tiddlies up and down the creek."

"Tiddlies?" Henry asked, "What are those?"

"Well, that's what we used to call icebergs. And when we found a good one we would tide it up the creek and back in the current. Of course my mother didn't like it much, but we never did fall in—just lucky, I guess. Anyway, you two be careful around the ice, now. It's all breaking up. I'll see you around," he said, picking up his bundle of wood and starting off across the marsh.

That night Henry stayed over, and as they slept Homer dreamed of icebergs—icebergs rising and falling with the tides, icebergs breaking loose from the edges of the marsh and floating in and out of the creek—under the bridge and past his house, drifting along in the warm, spring air. And then he dreamed that Mr. Birch was on an iceberg, too, leaning on a hoe and softly chuckling to himself as he floated along. "Running tiddlies, running tiddlies..." he kept saying. He and Henry were on an iceberg, and he could see his mother far away, on shore, waving to him and saying something he could not hear...

"I said good morning!" his mother said, throwing back the curtains of his room. "You two had better get up, now. It's a beautiful day." Henry was already up, pulling on his shoes, and from outside Homer could hear birds singing. When he kneeled on the bed and looked out he could see that the tide was rising, flowing swiftly under the bridge. They ate breakfast quickly, and then they were outside, running, all four running—Homer and Henry, Sophocles and Max—out across the road, over the bridge and onto the marsh as it stretched away in all directions, almost as far as the eye could see. The air was soft and warm, and there was no wind. They ran, and walked, and ran some more, the dogs sprinting out before them, noses to the ground as they chased after the scent of a deer that had passed there in the night.

A flock of ducks passed overhead with a soft whirring sound, and enormous pieces of ice, like beached whales, lay scattered across the marsh. Then they came to a place where they could go no farther, where the creek was too wide to cross, and an iceberg was wedged between the banks, like a bridge.

"Do you thinks it's safe?" Henry asked, but before Homer answered, Sophocles leaped, bounded off the ice and ran to the other side.

"It holds!" Homer cried, and the next thing he knew, he and Henry were standing on the iceberg, and as the tide rose, the iceberg rose with it. The two of them were floating, and with a long stick and a broken oar they had found, they pushed themselves down the canal, toward the swiftly moving water of the creek.

"Do you think we should?" Henry asked again. "The water's kind of cold, if we fell in."

Homer stomped down onto the iceberg with his foot, but it did not move. "We can always row to shore, if we have to." he said. But it was too late, anyway, for as they stood at the mouth of the creek, wondering if they should, or shouldn't, the current had already taken hold, pulled them a few yards away from shore and then upstream. As the two dogs barked from the shore, the boys were off, drifting up the river on a piece of ice, looking out across the marsh as the world passed by.

"Yippee!!" Homer cried, and Henry smiled. Then they just stood and watched, pulled along by the current. A single, puffy cloud floated overhead, and the house and the bridge grew smaller as the river bent and turned, disappearing altogether. The dogs bounded along the bank beside them, barking and then leaped into the river and swam to Homer and Henry. The two boys, with some difficulty, pulled them onboard. And then there were four—two dogs and two boys, drifting along in the soft yellow light of the sun.

"Look!" Henry said, pointing off to the edge of the woods where two deer, a mother and child, were standing.

"And over there!" Homer said, pointing to a tall, thin bird, a great blue heron, that was stalking along through the grass. The bird stopped, looked, and with a single flap of its wings, rose up and flew away. They looked back for the deer, but they, too, were gone. And then a flock of ducks passed overhead, wheeled once against the sky, and then swooped down and with a splashing sound settled into the creek nearby. Max and Sophocles watched, and whined softly.

Then a large, white cloud appeared and passed across the sun, and the air turned suddenly cool. A light wind sprang up, and what had seemed a warm day in May became a cold one in March. The two dogs, still wet from their swim, began to shiver and gaze off toward dry land. Suddenly they came into a part of the marsh where they had never been.

"How will we get home?" Homer wondered, but Henry had no answer.

"The tide will change, won't it?"

"It has to," said Homer, "but I don't know when."

More clouds appeared, the air grew colder, and then it happened—one flake, then another, slowly at first and then harder and harder until it was snowing so hard that they could not see. Soon the world turned to white, and caps of snow quickly formed, like hats, on the tops of all their heads. If they had been at home, safely on dry land, the two boys would have been happy, but as it was, trapped on an iceberg in a creek in the middle of the marsh, they were not. They could not even see the land, or the trees—only white.

Then, as quickly as it began, the snow slowed and, a moment later, stopped altogether. A patch of blue sky appeared, and then another. The sun came back out, and it was only then that they realized they were no longer moving, but standing perfectly still in the middle of the creek. Then they began to drift slowly back in the direction from which they had come.

"Yippee!" Homer said again, wiping the snow off his head and the two dogs. "The tide's turned."

And sure enough, as the sky turned blue again, the sun came back out, the snow melted on the surrounding marsh and the birds returned to the trees. The two boys drifted back in the direction from which they had come. Even the two dogs seemed happy, and stood up, staring expectantly downstream. As the current gathered speed, and the two boys looked happily out over the marsh in the warm spring air, they rounded a bend, and the house and the bridge appeared. In the distance they could see the red brick chimney of Mr. Birch's house, rising up through the trees.

"Heh," Homer wondered, suddenly. "How are we going to get to shore, anyway?"

"We'll row." Henry said, and with the broken paddle started to paddle to the shore. Homer joined him with the broken stick, but within a few minutes they were both exhausted, and had learned something about icebergs. They can't be rowed. They are too heavy, and the current was too strong, so no matter how hard they tried, they got no closer to shore.

"We'll be swept out to sea!" Homer said, starting to panic. As they rounded the last bend, and the current slowly gathered speed, they could hear the sound of rushing water as it passed under the bridge on its way out to the vast, salty reaches of the sea.

"Maybe we can swim for it." Henry said hopefully, but they both knew the water was too cold.

"We'll just have to stay on 'til someone sees us." Homer said and that was all they could do. As the bridge got closer and closer, and Max and Sophocles looked off toward the land and whined softly, and the sound of rushing water grew louder and louder, Homer felt as if he were about to cry. He wished he were in his backyard, on dry land, doing things other boys did on Saturday afternoons— running and jumping, playing soccer and throwing old, rotten apples.

But it was too late. "Hold on tight!" Henry said. The bridge was getting closer and closer, the iceberg was picking up speed and then they were under it, the water rolling up around them on all sides, the iceberg spinning along in the current like a cork, the sound of rushing water filling their ears.

And then they were through. "We made it!" they both shouted, and as the bridge grew smaller, they could hear another sound—the roaring of the surf from the sea. The dogs heard it too, and barked, and then barked some more. "We'll drown!" Homer cried, and then they heard another sound—of wood banging on wood, and when they looked around they saw an old rowboat coming toward them, and in it an old man with white hair, wearing a baseball cap, pulling hard at the oars.

"It's Mr. Birch!" Henry shouted. The old man glanced once over his shoulder, gave the oars another pull and the boat bumped up onto the iceberg. The two dogs jumped in.

"Good afternoon!" Mr. Birch said, cheerfully. "I thought you fellows might want a little help. It's a bit early in the year for a swim. Hop in! At this rate, we'll all be in Greenland for supper."

The boys climbed in, pushed off, and as Mr. Birch rowed, they watched as the iceberg floated away, downstream, and finally disappeared.

"I usually don't launch this old boat until May." he was saying, "But in your case I thought I'd make an exception. And I felt sort of responsible because I forgot to tell you boys something about icebergs— they can't be rowed. So if you're going for a ride, it's best to take a boat with you, just in case. I wanted to catch you before you went back under the bridge, but I'm not as young as I used to be, and it took a while to get this old boat in the creek."

"Thank you." Homer and Henry said, feeling kind of foolish. When they bumped up onto the marsh, they helped him pull up the boat.

"In any case, "Mr. Birch added, "All's well that ends well, but I guess running tiddlies is about over for this year. It's too warm. You boys better come into the house and dry off. Bring the dogs, too— they look kind of damp. My wife will want to see how all this turned out."

And so they all followed him down the road, and then along a narrow, winding path to the small, white house that sat nestled among the trees. Inside, he gave the two dogs each a bone, lit a fire in an old wood stove, and introduced them to his wife—a pretty woman with a braid of long white hair that reached halfway down her back. Homer and Henry took off their shoes and socks, and put them by the stove to dry. And as they sipped their hot milk, Mr. and Mrs. Birch told them stories of the olden days.

"And you boys come back to visit us, won't you?" she said when it was time to leave, and they promised they would. They woke up Max and Sophocles, who had fallen asleep by the fire, and pulled on their socks and shoes, which were still warm.

"And stay on dry land for a while, won't you boys?" Mr. Birch said. "I'm getting too old for this sort of thing."

"We will," they said, thanked them again, and went outside.

It was spring again. A warm sun shown down from a pale blue sky, birds were singing, and the dogs trotted along the road before them. Henry and Homer were too tired to run, and each picked up a long stick and tapped it along the path before them. When they reached the bridge they stopped and leaned on the rail and looked out over the marsh, but something had changed.

"What happened?" Henry wondered, but Homer did not answer. It was a moment before the two boys realized that there was not a speck of ice to be seen, for the last of the icebergs had been swept out to sea with the outgoing tide.

J
Updike, David.
A spring story $13.95